Shakespeare in a Nutshell

William Shakespeare
His Times
His Life
His Works

Shakespeare in Everyday Life
His Quotations

Written by
Leanne Mayo

Art by
Nicola Keane

Leanne Mayo

Second Edition 2010

Library of Congress Control Number: 2003097231

ISBN 0-9744868-1-7

King's Peak Publications
P. O. Box 910
Midway, Utah
84049
U. S. A.

Dedication

For My Family—

Raymond

Lisa, Michael, Dana,

Molly, Jeremy, Kimi

and

all

those

who

came

after

Acknowledgements

Special thanks to Raymond Mayo and Lisa Murphy for their counsel, assistance, and encouragement. Much appreciation to Evan Simper for his assistance. The efforts of my artist, Nicola Keane, and my editors, David and Kimball Richards, and Ben Schauerhamer, have been immeasurable. The completion of this book has been achieved because of this highly qualified support team. My gratitude extends to each one.

Part One: The Times, Life, and Works of William Shakespeare

Part Two: Shakespeare in Everyday Life
Quotations

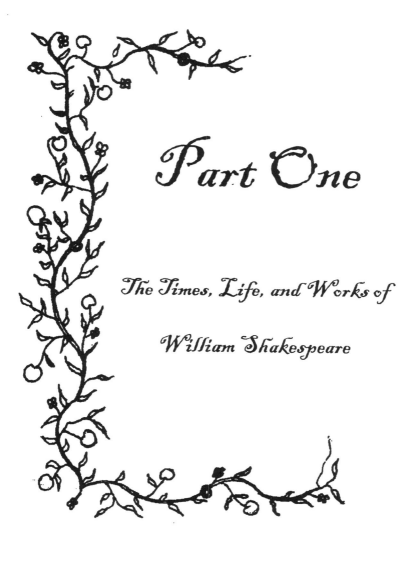

Part One

The Times, Life, and Works of

William Shakespeare

His Times

The Elizabethan Age

William Shakespeare was born during the spacious days
of Queen Elizabeth, known as the Elizabethan Age. It
was an era in which his genius could be fostered and
developed to the fullest. The religious strife of the
Reformation had eased. The fear of a Spanish conquest
had ended with the defeat of the Armada in 1588 at Calais
on the coast of France. English colonization was taking
place in the new world through the efforts of explorers
such as Drake, Raleigh, and Cabot. The Renaissance,
which began in the fourteenth century, nurtured and
increased learning and set the imaginations of men on
fire. The expanding horizons of the Englishmen's world
made them anxious to learn, love, feel, and experience all

they could. Drama was the art form that could bring the world to England. William Shakespeare was the genius who could give expression to this new and exciting and varied life.

Just what was everyday life like in Elizabethan Times?

Hygiene

Shakespeare's birthplace, Stratford on the River Avon, merry olde England, has a romantic ring to it. Picture beautiful gardens, lovely ladies, flowing dresses. However, everyday life in Stratford and London could be described in one word, dirty. People bathed only twice a year. There surely was some stench when attending the Globe Theater, where Shakespeare's plays were performed, as it was a day-long affair.

Baths were taken semi-annually in a big tub filled with hot water. The man of the house had the privilege of bathing first. Then the sons had their turn, followed by the other men in the household. Next the women and children used the same water. Last of all the babies were bathed. By then the water was so dirty someone could actually be lost in it. The saying, "don't throw the baby out with the bath water," really had meaning.

Mothers made sure between their spring and autumn baths that their children were coated with a protective layer of dirt. If a mother had to bathe her child, she would pray for his health until he could get another coating of dirt. It was a firmly held belief that water weakened one's constitution.

Most people got married in June because they took their baths in May and were still smelling pretty good. Just to be safe, brides carried a bouquet of flowers with them to hide their body odor. Thus, the traditions of June weddings and bridal flowers were begun.

Clothing

In the 1500's, the preferred mode of travel was by canal or riverboat when possible. Travel by road was filthy. Women's shoes were platforms with four metal bars connected at the base. They were generally six inches high. In Paris, these shoes became the fashion of the day reaching nearly one foot in height effectively keeping their pretty dresses out of the muck.

There were no buttons or zippers. People sewed themselves into their clothes. They remained in those clothes day and night for six months; then the semi-annual bath was taken, and they would sew themselves into a clean set of clothes befitting the season.

Hats were fashionable and necessary to protect their heads from creatures dropping out of the ceilings. These hats were known as skull caps. All the women, from the servants to the mistress of the house, wore these caps.

Home and Family

All the homes had thatched roofs. This was thick straw piled high with no wood underneath and no finished ceilings. It was the only place for animals to get warm; so all pets and other animals, such as dogs, cats, birds, mice, rats, and bugs, as well as their droppings, were in the loft. When it rained, it became slippery, and sometimes an animal would fall from his perch. Thus, the saying, "it's raining cats and dogs."

There was nothing to prevent things from falling from the thatch. This posed a real problem, especially in the bedroom. It could really mess up the nice clean bed. Going to bed alone did not ensure waking up alone; so beds were made with large posts and a sheet was hung over the top, the predecessors of our beautiful four poster beds with canopies.

But beds were few. Sometimes, just parents had beds. Generally, children and servants would simply sleep where they fell. William Shakespeare, wealthy in the Elizabethan class system, slept in a bed.

The floor in a lower-class home was dirt. These families were "dirt poor." The wealthy had slate floors which became slippery in the winter when wet; so thresh was spread on the floor to help them keep their footing. This thresh was made up of droppings, sticks, twigs, etc., and it was inhabited by little buggy creatures. It was matted down over time. When it stunk too badly, a layer of thresh was removed, and a new layer was added. It was sprinkled with wildflowers and herbs. This process was called "spring cleaning." As new thresh continued to be added, it would start slipping outside when the door was opened. A piece of wood was placed at the entry, creating a "threshold."

It was very dark in the homes with only one small window per room. This was intentional, as the people were taxed according to the amount of sunlight that entered the home.

A family's wealth was also judged by the amount of timber used in building the home, as it was very expensive.

Reeds dipped in wax were used as candles, giving off twenty minutes of light. If these were split the long way, they gave off twice as much light for ten minutes, burning the candle at both ends.

My candle burns at both ends,
It will not last the night.
But ah my foes and oh my friends,
It gives a lovely light.

Edna St. Vincent Millay

The "rule of thumb" meant that a man could beat his wife twice a day if he used a stick no bigger around than his thumb.

A pole with a bar extending from it was a baby tender. The baby was attached to the bar so he could encircle the pole. The baby's high chair had a hole in it, doubling as a potty chair and a high chair for feeding.

Food and Cooking

Water was kept in a big vat. A person used an average of three gallons a day because his work was generally hard labor and the salt content in food (their form of preservation) was very high. The master of the house wanted to be sure his servant was not drinking all the water; so he would typically say, "whistle while you bring the water." If a servant did drink, he "wet his whistle."

Homes that could afford kitchen maids referred to them as wenches. Cooking in the kitchen was done in a big kettle that always hung over the fire. Everyday the fire was lit, and new things were added to the pot. Meals consisted mainly of vegetables and a little meat. Stews were eaten for dinner, and leftovers remained in the pot to get cold overnight. These leftovers were the start of the next day's meal. Sometimes the stew had food in it that had been there for a month. Hence, the rhyme, "Peas porridge hot, peas porridge cold, peas porridge in the pot nine day old."

Sometimes pork was obtained, making an average day a special occasion. When company came over, the bacon was hung in plain view to show it off. It was a sign of wealth, illustrating that the man of the house could really "bring home the bacon." A piece of the meat was cut off to share with each guest, and all would sit around and "chew the fat."

Bread was divided according to status. Servants ate the burnt bottom of the loaf, family ate the middle, and guests were given the top, or the "upper crust."

Those with money had plates made of pewter. Lead from these plates tended to leach into foods with high acidity. This happened most often with tomatoes, leading people to believe they were poisonous. So they stopped eating them for 400 years! If someone were seen eating a tomato in the town square, people would stand around waiting to see if he would drop dead.

Most people did not have pewter plates, but trenchers. These were wooden boards with the middle scooped out like a bowl. They were never washed, and often worms got into the wood. After eating off wormy trenchers, a person might get "trench mouth."

In some households where there were no plates, the family table had two useable sides. When company came, the table was turned to the smooth side which was polished with beeswax. Daily meals were eaten on the rough side of the table. Food was placed directly into grooves carved in the surface of the wood. Lots of gravies were served, and bread was used to sop it up. The "sop" is still used to finish a meal in Europe today. There were no dishes to do! After eating, the table was returned to the shiny side until the next meal. This is the origin of the saying, "you turned the tables on me."

Out of charity, families kept a wooden box resembling a cage outside their door. It was used for their "baker's dozen" or leftovers. The poor, looking for a meal, would come and get them.

Romance

The terminology for dating was in accordance with the class system.

The lower class "wenched." A young man and woman might be seen wenching in the woods. The upper class "courted."

A young couple of the middle class was said to be "spooning." There was often a high-backed chair by the fireplace where the father sat in the evening hours. It was the warmest place. When a young man came to visit a young lady, he was given a piece of wood from which to whittle a spoon during his visit. Before he left, he was to give the spoon to her father. This would indicate his hands had been occupied and off the girl!

Death and Burial

Drinking cups were made of lead. The combination of
the lead with whiskey or ale could sometimes render a
drinker unconscious for a couple of days. He may have
been taken for dead and prepared for burial. By custom,
the dead person was laid out on the kitchen table for a
couple of days and the family gathered around, eating,
drinking, and waiting to see if perchance he would wake
up. Hence, the tradition of the "wake."

England is an island nation, old and small. Long ago,
space for burial started to become scarce. To
accommodate this problem, coffins were dug up and the
bones taken out, allowing the grave to be used again. In
reopening these coffins, one out of twenty-five were
found to have scratch marks on the inside of the lid.
People had been buried alive! To remedy this
unfortunate event, a string was tied on the corpse's wrist,

threaded through the coffin lid, up through the ground, and tied to a bell on the surface. Someone would have to sit out all night on the "graveyard shift" to listen for a "dead ringer" to be "saved by the bell."

His Life

William Shakespeare 1564-1616

His Personal Life

The Shakespeare family was not of the upper or aristocratic class. The father, John, was involved in agricultural pursuits. He was also a glover and served as mayor at one time as well. John was a man with good business sense, a self-made man. This was certainly rare in Elizabethan Times. Perhaps this background was an asset to William Shakespeare when it came time to market his plays. In later years, William had to come to the financial assistance of his family.

Shakespeare's mother, Mary Arden, is credited with bestowing her creativity upon her son. The Arden family was wealthier and owned more real estate than the Shakespeares. These two families were friends. Mary's family lived on the edge of the Arden forest. The forest was so thick that it was said a squirrel could scamper from end to end without ever touching the ground.

William was the third child in a family of eight—four boys and four girls. He had two older sisters who died in infancy. Two of the boys died very young. Only one sister, Joan, who married William Hart, has living descendants today, and they do not bear the Shakespeare name. William has none.

From age five, Shakespeare saw plays performed in Stratford by traveling groups of actors. His interest in theater likely started from a very young age.

The school that William probably attended in Stratford still stands. There are no lists of pupils left today. It was only for Freemen, the governing class. It is unusual that William would have the opportunity to attend. His genius and his father's position would have qualified him for admittance.

It is purported that when he reached his full stature, William was just five feet one inch tall!

William's wife was Anne Hathaway. Ann Hathaway's cottage still stands today. William married Anne when he was eighteen and she was twenty-six. She was pregnant at the time. They were married in November, 1582. Their daughter, Susanna, was born in May, 1583. Less than two years later, in February, 1585, twins Hamnet and Judith were born. Susanna married a doctor. Judith married a bartender and was disowned by her family, but one month before his death, Shakespeare altered his will to include her. Tragically, his only son, Hamnet, died at age eleven of an illness.

He was the father of three children two months before his twenty-first birthday. Even so, by the age of twenty-one, Shakespeare left Stratford for London to seek his career.

It is ninety miles between London and Stratford. He traveled back and forth, but probably not that frequently. When he returned to Stratford at age thirty-three, he bought the second largest home in town, New Place, in 1597. It cost him sixty pounds, which was a fortune in his day. It had been built by the Lord Mayor of London, Sir Hugh Clopton, one hundred years earlier. It had three stories, five gables, ten fireplaces, and fourteen rooms. It was built of brick and timber.

He still traveled to London and had dealings with actors and playwrights. He returned in 1610 to retire at age forty-six. By then he had made further purchases in Stratford, thus building up his estate including arable, pasture, and garden land. He would have been considered wealthy. Records in Stratford show that he became involved in community life.

When he died, William left New Place to his daughter, Susanna, and her husband, John Hall. It is likely that William's widow lived with them till her death, as widows just went along with the furniture. William's granddaughter, Elizabeth Hall, owned New Place after her parents' death. Only the foundation of New Place stands today. It is preserved with gardens around it. Behind it stands Nash House. The granddaughter's first husband was Thomas Nash. Chronicles, remedies, and tools are on exhibit at Hall's Croft. These belonged to Elizabeth's father, Dr. John Hall. William's granddaughter, Elizabeth, was an only child and had no children. William's daughter, Judith, had three sons who died at ages one, nineteen, and twenty-one, and had no issue. They would not have borne the Shakespeare name.

William died in 1616, at the age of fifty-two, probably on his birthday, April 23rd. He died of a fever after a ninety mile ride on horseback in the March rain from London to Stratford. Tradition has it that he had a drink with friends upon arrival, contracted the fever, possibly pneumonia, and died a short time later. It was a week after the burial of his brother-in-law, William Hart, Joan's husband.

His headstone reads:

> *Good friends for Jesus sake, forbear*
> *To dig the dust enclosed here.*
> *Blessed be ye man who spares these stones,*
> *And cursed be he who moves my bones.*

And bones and graves were disturbed in those times!! To be sure his bones were not disturbed, William was buried fifteen feet deep.

His wife, Anne, died at the age of sixty-seven in the year 1623. She was eight years older than William and lived seven years after he died; so her lifespan was fifteen years longer.

Shakespeare is remembered each year in Stratford on the anniversary of his birth and death day, April 23rd. Among other events, a floral procession makes its way from his birthplace to the poet's tomb which is under the floor and in front of the altar in Holy Trinity Church in Stratford. It was the same church in which he had been christened.

His Professional Life

William left Stratford in his twenty-first year and walked to London by way of Oxford.

He started in the theater as a call boy or page. Next, he became an actor. He was prominent in the theater world by the age of twenty-eight. He owned his own theater company and was a business success. He made a tremendous impact on London and on the world.

Remember, London was ready for this renewed and blossoming art form in the re-awakened world of people hungry for knowledge and self-expression.

The Globe Theater

The theater was held in the daytime in the open air, as there were no lights or electricity. It was like a theater in the round; and it has been called the wooden O. It was very informal. Peasants, called groundlings, surrounded the stage. The rich people, called gallants and courtiers, were in the tiers. All the seats were good. Spectators were involved. It was as if they were eavesdropping on the play. The players would go to the edge of the stage to talk to the audience. Since there was no darkened theater, only daylight, everyone could be seen. There were no special effects, not even trap doors. If a player died, he would just be on the stage for the remainder of the play. He could not just walk off!

His Works

In the Workshop

This was the period in which William experimented, imitated, and adapted. There was so much ardor and beauty in the world, and what Shakespeare borrowed, he made it his own. Plays in this period include:

> *Titus Andronicus*
> *Two Gentlemen of Verona*
> *Romeo and Juliet*

Romeo and Juliet was the first play to show the promise of his full power. He wrote it at the age of thirty-three in 1597.

In the World

In this period, he wrote histories and comedies. The best of this series of work was perhaps *Henry IV*. He gathered information for these plays from *Holingshed's Chronicles of England, Scotland, and Ireland, 1597.*

Some of his favorite characters in this period were Falstaff, Beatrice, Portia, and Viola.

Out of the Depths

This was Shakespeare's somber, philosophic period, but he was not morbid. Beginning about 1600, his plays became darker and more intense. His son, Hamnet, had died in 1595, at age eleven. Some of the plays he wrote during this period are:

His Works

Hamlet

Macbeth

King Lear

Othello

On the Heights

During these last six years of William's writing career, his
plays exhibited wisdom and a more genial outlook. These
were his mellowing years. He was a moderately rich man
and traveled between Stratford and London. Plays in this
period include:

The Tempest

Cymbeline

A Winter's Tale

Summary

Plays were kept in manuscript form, and people who wanted to become acquainted with a writer's drama had to attend the play itself. Most people could not read anyway. Books were few. People knew mostly about the Bible. Therefore, by 1623, only sixteen of William's plays had been printed. He had died in 1616, seven years before.

In addition to his thirty-seven plays, Shakespeare composed 154 sonnets. These were short rhymed poems of fourteen lines each. They are considered the noblest lyrics in the language. Also, he wrote several longer poems.

Shakespeare's works have the outstanding quality of universality. They reached out to everyone. He had a universal mind.

His Works

Four of William's major resources were his:

- Love of nature
- History books about the lives of English royalty
- Knowledge of country folklore
- Greek & Roman Classics

Cymbeline is an example of his use of country folklore. It contains many of the elements in the story of *Snow White*. His frequent use of flowers in his poetry is a fine example of his love of nature.

From these four springboards came the world's greatest poet and playwright. He wrote two plays a year with ease. His works have been translated into all modern languages.

Through the years that Shakespeare wrote, his power as a playwright grew. His depth and emotion increased. He was the supreme dramatist of the world.

William was able to combine these three qualities that make literature enduring:

- He presented human frailties with the wisdom to understand and the charity to forgive.

- He presented human nature with both realism and idealism at the same time.

- He displayed the range of emotions from light-heartedness and laughter to pity and passion.

The music of his verse was charming to the ear. Indeed, some of the world's most beautiful melodies have been written to accompany his plays.

His Works

His masterpieces were given to the world with ease and careless grace.

Ben Jonson was a famous literary figure and one of the friends with whom Shakespeare had a merry meeting the night he became ill. Jonson probably wrote more about Shakespeare than anyone else. After William's death, Jonson said of him:

He was not of an age, but for all time.

"... good phrases are surely,

and ever were,

very commendable. "

King Henry IV (Act 3 Scene 2)

Part Two

Shakespeare in Everyday Life

- Quotations from his Works

Personal Behavior

Circle of Life

After All

Personal

Behavior

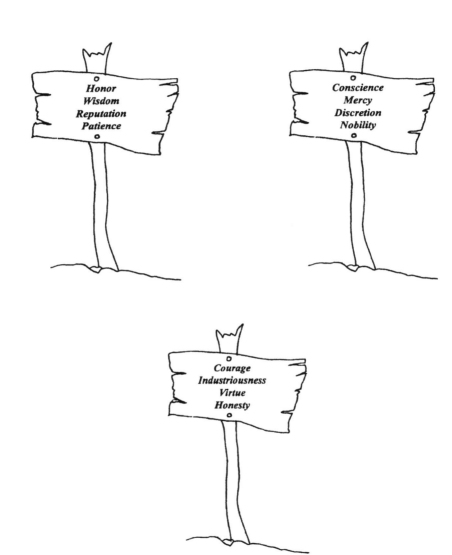

Character Building Qualities

In thy face I see
The map of honour,
Truth, and loyalty.

> **The Second Part of King Henry VI**
> **(Act 3, Scene 1)**

O Lord! That lends me life,
Lend me a heart replete with thankfulness.

> **The Second Part of King Henry VI**
> **(Act 1, Scene 1)**

God be prais'd, that to believing souls
Gives light in darkness, comfort in despair!

> **The Second Part of King Henry VI**
> **(Act 2, Scene 1)**

I will be the pattern of all patience.

> **The Tragedy of King Lear (Act 3, Scene 2)**

This above all: to thine own self be true.
And it must follow, as the night the day,
Thou cans't not then be false to any man.

The Tragedy of Hamlet (Act 1, Scene 3)

What a piece of work is man!
How noble in reason!
How infinite in faculty!
In form and moving how express and admirable!
In action how like an angel!
In apprehension how like a god!

The Tragedy of Hamlet (Act 2, Scene 2)

Men should be what they seem.

The Tragedy of Othello (Act 3, Scene 3)

The better part of valour is discretion.

**The First Part of King Henry IV
(Act 5, Scene 4)**

There is a tide in the affairs of men,
Which taken at the flood, leads on to fortune.
Omitted, all the voyage of their life
Is bound in shallows and in miseries.

The Tragedy of Julius Caesar (Act 4, Scene 3)

Mine honour is my life; both grow in one;
Take honour from me, and my life is done.

**The Tragedy of King Richard II
(Act 1, Scene 1)**

No legacy is so rich as honesty.

All's Well That Ends Well (Act 3, Scene 5)

But if it be a sin to covet honour,
I am the most offending soul alive.

The Life of Henry V (Act 4, Scene 3)

True nobility is exempt from fear.

**The Second Part of King Henry VI
(Act 4, Scene 1)**

How beauteous mankind is!
O brave new world,
That hath such people in't!

The Tempest (Act 5, Scene 1)

For courage mounteth with occasion.

**The Life and Death of King John
(Act 2, Scene 1)**

How poor are they that have not patience!

The Tragedy of Othello (Act 2, Scene 3)

A peace above all earthly dignities,
A still and quiet conscience.

The Life of King Henry VIII (Act 3, Scene 2)

Virtue is bold, and goodness never fearful.

Measure of Measure (Act 3, Scene 1)

Assume a virtue, if you have it not.

The Tragedy of Hamlet (Act 3, Scene 4)

To be honest, as this world goes, is to be one man picked out of ten thousand.

The Tragedy of Hamlet (Act 2, Scene 2)

From lowest place when virtuous things proceed,
The place is dignified by the doer's deed.

All's Well That Ends Well (Act 2, Scene 3)

You may say that's a valiant flea that dare eat his breakfast on the lip of a lion.

The Life of Henry V (Act 3, Scene 7)

Our bodies are our gardens, to the which our wills are gardeners;
Either to have it sterile with idleness or manured with industry.

The Tragedy of Othello (Act 1, Scene 3)

Who is it that says most? Which can say more
Than this rich praise, that you alone are you?

Sonnet LXXXIV

I am a true labourer: I earn that I eat, get that I wear,
Owe no man hate, envy no man's happiness,
Glad of other men's good.

As You Like It (Act 3, Scene 2)

Who steals my purse steals trash; 'tis something,
Nothing;
'Twas mine, 'tis his, and had been slave to thousands;
But he that filches from me my good name
Robs me of that which not enrichens him,
And makes me poor indeed.

The Tragedy of Othello (Act 3, Scene 3)

Sweet mercy is nobility's true badge.

**The Tragedy of Titus Andronicus
(Act 1, Scene 1)**

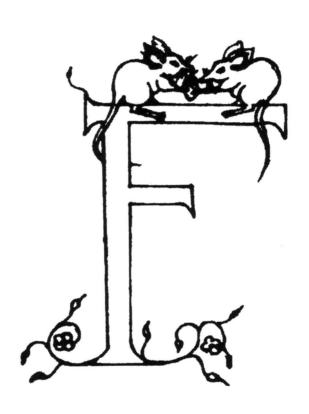

Friendship

I count myself in nothing else so happy
As in a soul remembering my good friends.

The Tragedy of Richard III (Act 2, Scene 3)

I'll note you in my book of memory.

**The First Part of King Henry VI
(Act 2, Scene 4)**

We are advertis'd by our loving friends.

**The Third Part of King Henry VI
(Act 5, Scene 3)**

But if the while I think on thee, dear friend,
All losses are restor'd and sorrows end.

Sonnet XXX

Fools

I had rather have a fool to make me merry than experience to make me sad.

As You Like It (Act 4, Scene 1)

He has not so much brain as ear-wax.

The Tragedy of Troilus and Cressida (Act 5, Scene 1)

The fool doth think he is wise, but the wise man knows himself to be a fool.

As You Like It (Act 5, Scene 1)

Foolery, sir, does walk about the orb like the sun; it shines everywhere.

Twelfth Night (Act 3, Scene 1)

The little foolery that wise men have makes a great show.

As You Like It (Act 1, Scene 2)

Always the dullness of the fool is the whetstone of the wits.

As You Like It (Act 1, Scene 2)

Better a witty fool than a foolish wit.

Twelfth Night (Act 1, Scene 5)

Food

Who risest from a feast
With that keen appetite that he sits down?

The Merchant of Venice (Act 2, Scene 6)

Unquiet meals make ill digestions.

The Comedy of Errors (Act 5, Scene 1)

Appetite, a universal wolf.

**The Tragedy of Troilus and Cressida
(Act 1, Scene 3)**

Now, good digestion wait on appetite,
And health on both!

The Tragedy of Macbeth (Act 3, Scene 4)

Talking

Have more than thou showest,
Speak less than thou knowest.

The Tragedy of King Lear (Act 1, Scene 4)

Brevity is the soul of wit.

The Tragedy of Hamlet (Act 2, Scene 2)

No word like pardon.

**The Tragedy of King Richard II
(Act 5, Scene 3)**

Ill deeds are doubled with an evil word.

The Comedy of Errors (Act 3, Scene 2)

I would my horse had the speed of your tongue, and so good a continuer.

Much Ado About Nothing (Act 1, Scene 1)

My words fly up, my thoughts remain below:
Words without thoughts never to heaven go.

The Tragedy of Hamlet (Act 3, Scene 3)

Give thy thoughts no tongue.

The Tragedy of Hamlet (Act 1, Scene 3)

Society is no comfort
To one not sociable.

The Tragedy of Cymbeline (Act 4, Scene 2)

Keep a good tongue in your head.

The Tempest (Act 3, Scene 2)

I had a thing to say.
But I will fit it with some better time.

**The Life and Death of King John
(Act 3, Scene 3)**

The deep of night is crept upon our talk,
And nature must obey necessity.

The Tragedy of Julius Caesar (Act 4, Scene 3)

Harp not on that string.

The Tragedy of Richard III (Act 4, Scene 4)

And yet words are no deeds.

The Life of King Henry VIII (Act 3, Scene 2)

An honest tale speeds best being plainly told.

The Tragedy of Richard III (Act 4, Scene 4)

Two may keep counsel when the third's away.

**The Tragedy of Titus Andronicus
(Act 4, Scene 2)**

Talkers are no good doers.

The Tragedy of Richard III (Act 1, Scene 3)

Circle

of

Life

Women

So far as my coin would stretch; and where it would not, I have used my credit.

**The First Part of King Henry IV
(Act 1, Scene 2)**

A woman is a dish for the gods.

**The Tragedy of Anthony and Cleopatra
(Act 5, Scene 2)**

Great with child, and longing for stewed prunes.

Measure of Measure (Act 2, Scene 1)

Do you not know I am a woman? When I think, I must speak.

As You Like It (Act 3, Scene 2)

Kindness in women, not their beauteous looks,
Shall win my love.

The Taming of the Shrew (Act 4, Scene 2)

The lady doth protest too much, methinks.

The Tragedy of Hamlet (Act 3, Scene 2)

How hard it is for women to keep counsel.

The Tragedy of Julius Caesar (Act 2, Scene 4)

Have you not heard it said full oft,
A woman's nay doth stand for naught.

Sonnets to Sundry Notes of Music XIX

A light wife doth make a heavy husband.

The Merchant of Venice (Act 5, Scene 1)

Her voice was ever soft,
Gentle, and low, an excellent thing in woman.

The Tragedy of King Lear (Act 5, Scene 2)

There's language in her eye, her cheek, her lip.

The Tragedy of Troilus and Cressida (Act 4, Scene 5)

Frailty, thy name is woman!

The Tragedy of Hamlet (Act 1, Scene 2)

Wives may be merry, and yet honest too.

The Merry Wives of Windsor (Act 4, Scene 2)

Men

I could not endure a husband with a beard on his face;
I had rather lie in the woollen.

Much Ado About Nothing (Act 2, Scene 1)

They say an old man is twice a child.

The Tragedy of Hamlet (Act 2, Scene 2)

He was a man
Of an unbounded stomach.

The Life of King Henry VIII (Act 4, Scene 2)

Men of few words are the best men.

The Life of Henry V (Act 3, Scene 2)

There is a history in all men's lives.

**The Second Part of King Henry IV
(Act 3, Scene 1)**

Sigh no more, ladies, sigh no more,
Men were deceivers ever,
One foot in sea and one on shore;
To one thing constant never.

Much Ado About Nothing (Act 2, Scene 3)

What he hath scanted men in hair, he hath given them in wit.

Comedy of Errors (Act 2, Scene 2)

Love, Marriage

Love comforteth like sunshine after rain.

Venus and Adonis

For thy sweet love remember'd such wealth brings
That then I scorn to change my state with kings.

Sonnet XXIX

But love is blind, and lovers cannot see
The pretty follies that themselves commit.

The Merchant of Venice (Act 2, Scene 6)

Base men being in love have then a nobility in their
natures more than is native to them.

The Tragedy of Othello (Act 2, Scene 1)

To kill a wife with kindness.

The Taming of the Shrew (Act 4, Scene 1)

Love sought is good, but given unsought, is better.

Twelfth Night (Act 3, Scene 1)

They do not love that do not show their love.

The Two Gentlemen of Verona (Act 1, Scene 2)

Hasty marriage seldom proveth well.

The Third Part of King Henry VI (Act 4, Scene 1)

Then let thy love be younger than thyself,
Or thy affection cannot hold the bent.

Twelfth Night (Act 2, Scene 4)

My bounty is as boundless as the sea,
My love as deep; the more I give to thee
The more I have, for both are infinite.

The Tragedy of Romeo and Juliet (Act 2, Scene 2)

No sooner met but they looked;
No sooner looked but they loved;
No sooner loved but they sighed;
No sooner sighed but they asked one another the reason;
No sooner knew the reason but they sought the remedy.

As You Like It (Act 5, Scene 2)

Though last, not least in love.

The Tragedy of Julius Caesar (Act 3, Scene 1)

For aught that I could ever read,
Could ever hear by tale or history,
The course of true love never did run smoothly.

A Midsummer Night's Dream (Act 1, Scene 1)

The wound invisible
That love's keen arrows make.

As You Like It (Act 3, Scene 5)

Let me not to the marriage of true minds
Admit impediments. Love is not love
Which alters when it alteration finds.

Sonnet CXVI

And ruin'd love, when it is built anew,
Grows fairer than at first, more strong, far greater.

Sonnet CXIX

Though last, not least in love.

The Tragedy of Julius Caesar (Act 3, Scene 1)

A young man married is a man that's marr'd.

All's Well That Ends Well (Act 2, Scene 3)

Children, Youth, Age

How sharper than a serpent's tooth it is
To have a thankless child!

The Tragedy of King Lear (Act 1, Scene 4)

It is a wise father that knows his own child.

The Merchant of Venice (Act 2, Scene 2)

Then come kiss me, sweet and twenty,
Youth's a stuff will not endure.

Twelfth Night (Act 2, Scene 3)

Crabbed age and youth cannot live together.
Youth is full of pleasure, age is full of cure.

The Passionate Pilgrim XII

Grief Sorrow, Death

What's gone and what's past help
Should be past grief.

The Winter's Tale (Act 3, Scene 2)

When sorrows come,
they come not single spies,
But in battalions.

The Tragedy of Hamlet (Act 4, Scene 5)

Everyone can master a grief but he that has it.

Much Ado About Nothing (Act 3, Scene 2)

By medicine life may be prolong'd yet death
Will seize the doctor too.

The Tragedy of Cymbeline (Act 5, Scene 5)

The bitter past, more welcome is the sweet.

All's Well That Ends Well (Act 5, Scene 3)

What is pomp, rule, reign, but earth and dust?
And, live we how we can, yet die we must.

**The Third Part of King Henry VI
(Act 5, Scene 2)**

Death's a great disguiser.

Measure for Measure (Act 4, Scene 2)

Every cloud engenders not a storm.

**The Third Part of King Henry VI
(Act 5, Scene 3)**

How much better is it to weep at joy than to joy in weeping.

Much Ado About Nothing (Act 1, Scene 1)

One woe doth tread upon another's heel,
So fast they follow.

The Tragedy of Hamlet (Act 4, Scene 7)

Affliction may one day smile again; and till then, sit thee down, sorrow!

Love's Labour's Lost (Act 1, Scene 1)

To weep is to make less the depth of grief.

**The Third Part of King Henry VI
(Act 2, Scene 1)**

Patch grief with proverbs.

Much Ado About Nothing (Act 5, Scene 1)

...rather bear those ills we have
Than fly to others that we know not of.

The Tragedy of Hamlet (Act 3, Scene 1)

After
All

Truisms

Fortune brings in some boats that are not steer'd.

The Tragedy of Cymbeline (Act 4, Scene 3)

He is well paid that is well satisfied.

The Merchant of Venice (Act 4, Scene 1)

There's a time for all things.

The Comedy of Errors (Act 2, Scene 2)

Condemn the fault, and not the actor of it?

Measure for Measure (Act 2, Scene 2)

How use doth breed a habit in man!

The Two Gentlemen of Verona (Act 5, Scene 4)

Self-love, my liege, is not so vile a sin
As self-neglecting.

The Life of Henry V (Act 2, Scene 4)

And oftentimes excusing of a fault
Doth make the fault the worse by the excuse.

The Life and Death of King John
(Act 4, Scene 2)

Master, I marvel how the fishes live in the sea.
Why, as men do aland; the great ones eat up the little
ones.

Pericles, Prince of Tyre (Act 2, Scene 1)

Great floods have flown
From simple sources.

All's Well That Ends Well (Act 2, Scene 1)

If all the year were playing holidays,
To sport would be as tedious as to work.

The First Part of King Henry IV
(Act 1, Scene 2)

We know what we are, but know not what we may be.

The Tragedy of Hamlet (Act 4, Scene 5)

The cock, that is the trumpet of the morn.

The Tragedy of Hamlet (Act 1, Scene 1)

Rubbing the poor itch of your opinion,
Make yourselves scabs.

The Tragedy of Coriolanus (Act 1, Scene 1)

Men prize the thing ungain'd more than it is.

**The Tragedy of Troilus and Cressida
(Act 1, Scene 2)**

Heat not a furnace for your foe so hot
That it do singe yourself.

The Life of King Henry VIII (Act 1, Scene 1)

Small things make base men proud.

The Second Part of King Henry VI
(Act 4, Scene 1)

How bitter a thing it is to look into happiness through another man's eyes.

As You Like It (Act 4, Scene 2)

Receive what cheer you may:
The night is long that never finds the day.

The Tragedy of Macbeth (Act 4, Scene 3)

With devotion's visage
And pious action we do sugar o'er
The devil himself.

The Tragedy of Hamlet (Act 3, Scene 1)

Welcome ever smiles,
And farewell goes out sighing.

The Tragedy and Troilus and Cressida
(Act 3, Scene 3)

Rich gifts wax poor when givers prove unkind.

The Tragedy of Hamlet (Act 3, Scene 1)

The web of our life is of a mingled yarn, good and ill
together.

All's Well That Ends Well (Act 4, Scene 3)

A little fire is quickly trodden out;
Which, being suffered, rivers cannot quench.

The Third Part of King Henry VI
(Act 4, Scene 8)

Famous Sayings

Child Rowland to the dark tower came.
His ward was still, Fie, fah, and fum.
I smell the blood of a British man.

The Tragedy of King Lear (Act 3, Scene 4)

As cold as any stone.

The Life of Henry V (Act 2, Scene 3)

Both of you are birds of a self-same feather.

The Third Part of King Henry VI (Act 3, Scene 3)

All's well that ends well.

All's Well That Ends Well (Act 4, Scene 4)

A horse! A horse! My kingdom for a horse!

The Tragedy of Richard III (Act 5, Scene 4)

Having nothing, nothing can he lose.

The Third Part of Henry VI (Act 3, Scene 3)

He hath eaten me out of house and home.

**The Second Part of King Henry I
(Act 2, Scene 1)**

Smooth runs the water where the brook is deep.

**The Second Part of King Henry VI
(Act 3, Scene 1)**

What! Is the old king dead?
As nail in door.

**The Second Part of King Henry IV
(Act 5, Scene 3)**

This house is turned upside down.

**The First Part of King Henry IV
(Act 2, Scene 1)**

Truth it is that we have seen better days.

As You Like It (Act 2, Scene 7)

Pray you now, forget and forgive.

The Tragedy of King Lear (Act 4, Scene 7)

Now is the winter of our discontent
Made glorious summer by this sun of York.

The Tragedy of Richard III (Act 1, Scene 1)

I am tied to the stake, and I must stand the course.

The Tragedy of King Lear (Act 3, Scene 7)

Beware the ides of March.

The Tragedy of Julius Caesar (Act 1, Scene 2)

Double, double toil and trouble.
Fire burn and cauldron bubble.

The Tragedy of Macbeth (Act 4, Scene 1)

Yet do I fear thy nature;
It is too full o' the milk of human kindness.

The Tragedy of Macbeth (Act 1, Scene 5)

Though this be madness, yet there is method in't.

The Tragedy of Hamlet (Act 2, Scene 2)

 Give every man thy ear,
But few thy voice;
Take each man's censure,
But reserve thy judgment.
Costly thy habit as thy purse can buy,
But not express'd in fancy; rich, not gaudy;
For the apparel oft proclaims the man.

The Tragedy of Hamlet (Act 1, Scene 3)

Nothing will come of nothing.

The Tragedy of King Lear (Act 1, Scene 2)

I have not slept one wink.

The Tragedy of Cymbeline (Act 3, Scene 4)

One for all, or all for one we gage.

The Rape of Lucrece

That's neither here nor there.

The Merry Wives of Windsor (Act 1, Scene 4)

It makes us, or it mars us.

The Tragedy of Othello (Act 5, Scene 1)

Things without all remedy
Should be without regard; what's done is done.

The Tragedy of Macbeth (Act 3, Scene 2)

The game is up.

The Tragedy of Cymbeline (Act 3, Scene 3)

O! beware, my lord, of jealousy;
It is the green-eyed monster which doth mark
The meat it feeds on.

The Tragedy of Othello (Act 3, Scene 3)

Let Hercules himself do what he may,
The cat will mew and dog will have his day.

The Tragedy of Hamlet (Act 5, Scene 1)

What's mine is yours, and what is yours is mine.

Measure of Measure (Act 5, Scene 1)

Neither rhyme nor reason.

As You Like It (Act 3, Scene 2)

Every why hath a wherefore.

The Comedy of Errors (Act 2, Scene 2)

Poor harmless fly.

**The Tragedy of Titus Andronicus
(Act 3, Scene 2)**

Speak low, if you speak love.

Much Ado About Nothing (Act 2, Scene 1)

Lord, what fools these mortals be!

A Midsummer Night's Dream (Act 3, Scene 2)

All that glitters is not gold.

The Merchant of Venice (Act 2, Scene 7)

In the twinkling of an eye.

The Merchant of Venice (Act 2, Scene 2)

A good heart's worth gold.

**The Second Part of King Henry IV
(Act 2, Scene 4)**

He will give the devil his due.

**The First Part of King Henry IV
(Act 1, Scene 2)**

My purpose is, indeed, a horse of that colour.

Twelfth Night (Act 2, Scene 3)

Laugh yourself into stitches.

Twelfth Night (Act 3, Scene 2)

The play's the thing
Wherein I'll catch the conscience of the king.

The Tragedy of Hamlet (Act 2, Scene 2)

You tread upon my patience.

The First Part of King Henry IV
(Act 1, Scene 3)

This is the short and the long of it.

The Merry Wives of Windsor (Act 2, Scene 2)

After All

And thus we see
that in the course of five hundred years
we have carried forward traditions
and have not changed very much.

About the Artist

Nicola Keane comes from a rich heritage of artistic talent. She is from Dewsbury, Yorkshire, England, and she is currently living in Scotland. She attended Arbroath College where she earned an HNC in Fine Art.

About the Author

Leanne Mayo was born and grew up in California. She attended San Jose State University and graduated from Brigham Young University. She has taught in both public and private schools. She is married to Raymond Mayo. They are the parents of six children and the grandparents of twelve. She has had a lifelong love for and appreciation of the fine arts. She has studied art history and has been a docent at the Utah Museum of Fine Arts at the University of Utah for ten years. She has spoken to literary, school, and women's groups from British Columbia to Georgia. She shares the biographies and works of famous literary figures, including William Shakespeare.